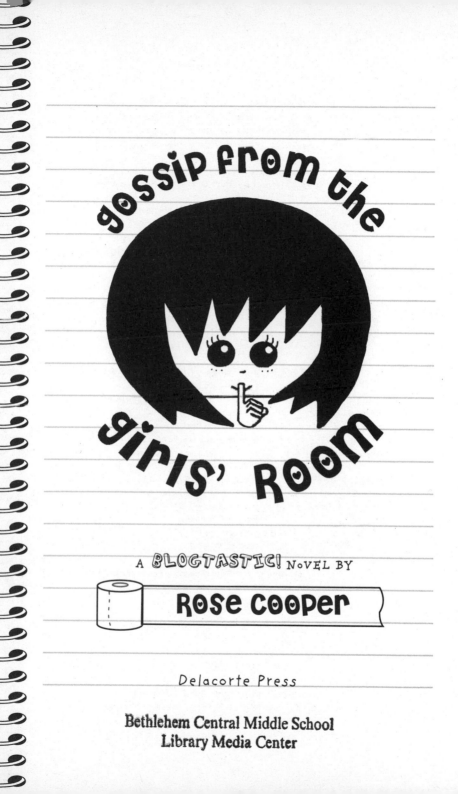

gossip from the girls' Room

A *BLOGTASTIC!* NOVEL BY

ROSE COOPER

Delacorte Press

Copyright © 2011 by Rose Cooper
Cover illustration copyright © 2011 by Rose Cooper

Delacorte Press is a registered trademark and the colophon is a trademark
of Random House, Inc.

Visit us on the Web! www.randomhouse.com/kids

Educators and librarians, for a variety of teaching tools, visit us at
www.randomhouse.com/teachers

Library of Congress Cataloging-in-Publication Data
Cooper, Rose.
Blogtastic! : gossip from the girls' room / by Rose Cooper. — 1st ed.
p. cm.
Summary: Sixth-grader Sofia Becker writes a blog about everything she
overhears in the girls' bathroom, especially mean things about the
super-popular Mia, but comes to realize that gossip has consequences
and popularity is hard to achieve.
ISBN 978-0-385-73947-4 (trade)—ISBN 978-0-375-89765-8 (ebook)
[1. Gossip—Fiction. 2. Blogs—Fiction. 3. Popularity—Fiction. 4. Middle
schools—Fiction. 5. Schools—Fiction.] I. Title.
PZ7.C78768 Blo
[Fic]—dc22
2009053658

The text of this book is set in 12-point Providence-Sans.

Book design by Marci Senders

Printed in the United States of America
10 9

First Edition

To my son, Christian.

Thank you for being such an inspiration.

I love you.

ACKNOWLEDGMENTS

I'm very lucky to have friends and family who have supported my lifelong dream of becoming a writer. I appreciate and love all of you. There are some individuals I'd like to give an extra-special thank-you to:

My fabulous agent, Rosemary Stimola, who helped make my dream into a reality. I can't thank you enough.

Wendy Loggia, editor extraordinaire. I'm incredibly lucky for being able to work with someone as hardworking and dedicated as you.

My fantastic designer, Marci Senders. You made working together fun, and I couldn't imagine working with any designer but you. Thank you for all your patience.

Krista Vitola, Wendy's right-hand person, and the hardworking team at Random House who helped bring this book to life.

My husband, Carl, who believed in me and gave me all the time I needed to write. I could not have done this without your support. And my boys, Christian, Alexander, and Sammy: your smiling faces always keep me going.

My mom, Kim. Your encouragement and your teaching me to never give up have made me who I am today. I love you.

Novel Idea—Mindy Alyse Weiss, Annmarie Myers, Deb Marshall, Judith Mammay, and Niki Moss. Besides being a wonderful critique group, you are amazing, talented writers and I'm lucky to call you my friends. Thank you for sharing this entire experience with me. I don't know where I would be without you.

And to the real-life Nona Bows, Rachael Taylor-Sorenson. Your constant humor and nonsense rambling have kept me inspired. You rock!

WARNING!!!

This is not just any notebook. This is my Pre-Blogging Notebook. My innermost private thoughts, until most of them become public the next day on my almost-popular blog. I know, I know, most people don't need a pre-blogging notebook. But _I_ am not most people. _I_ need to jot down all the juiciness, since my brain sometimes goes numb. I don't want to forget any single super-important details. Or get them mixed up when I actually blog about them. That might cause problems.

This notebook is so super-secret that it is cleverly disguised as a regular, ordinary, everyday boring notebook. And _NOBODY_ knows of its very existence.

Except for Nona. She's my BFF so that makes her an exception and the only one in the whole universe.

By the way, if you are holding my notebook

{1}

(which makes you the #2 person in the universe) you are breaking the law that prohibits snooping people such as yourself from reading other people's pre-blogging thoughts. So if I were you and for the sake of your health I highly recommend you consider the consequences of your nosy actions.

That's right, put the notebook down and slooowly back away. . . .

MONDAY

01

gossip from the girls' Room

Katie told Amber that Megan cheated on the big math test. Amber said the answers were written on Megan's shoe!

I couldn't help but accidentally overhear gossip in the girls' room today. Mia St. Claire and Alissa were talking (actually, they were whispering, so I had to overhear very carefully). They didn't realize I was in the far left bathroom stall, the one at the very, very end. The reason they didn't know I was in that very last stall, aside from me being super-discreet, is that NOBODY ever goes in there. On purpose. Ever since someone stunk up that stall really, horribly bad three months ago. And everyone knows that it's still stink-haunted.

The only reason I, Sofia Becker, used that Stink-Haunted Stall is because all of the other stalls were occupied and I really had no choice. It was either that or take the chance of being called Puddles the rest of my sixth-grade life. And possibly seventh.

CHOICE A	CHOICE B
Stink-Haunted Peer Pressure	Ruin social life forever with "Puddles" nickname

Pick me! Pick me!

Clearly, the choice was obvious.

Mia St. Claire is only THE most popular girl in all of Middlebrooke Middle School, for three very obvious reasons:

1. She's very rich and annoyingly pretty.

2. She has tons of money.

3. She can buy anything and everything she wants. And she does.

I'm sure people like her for other reasons too, but none of those reasons are obvious enough for me to really know. Or care about, for that matter.

Possibly a working brain?

Big puppy-dog eyes

Cutsie bow
(gag!)

So not jealous
of this dimple

Biggest smile.
EVER.

Long luxurious
locks

Maybe a (good) personality?

This is my non-caring face, see?

Even though it's only our first year of middle
school, Mia transferred her popularity from
elementary school. Who knew popularity was
transferable? Apparently, so is non-popularity.

{6}

But I have decided why Mia should be the most unpopular girl in all of Middlebrooke Middle School. For three very smart and intelligent reasons:

1. She has so much money she probably blows her nose with it. How gross is that?

Ewww! I really am totally gross. I'm so glad Sofia made me realize it. She is so übercool!

2. I am way prettier than her. Even though nobody else thinks so. Except my BFF, Nona. And my

{7}

parrot, Sam Sam. Even though I might have trained him to whistle at me and call me beautiful. Actually, I barely even remember teaching him that.

Mia is a dummy!

Sofia is prettier than Mia. Squawk!

(I also didn't teach him to say that.)

3. Mia acts like being super-pretty and totally rich doesn't matter or something. Everyone knows it's just an act to rub our noses in her fantasticness.

And really, what kind of a name is Mia St. Claire? "St." is the abbreviation for street. And "Claire" is a girl's first name. See what I mean? I think it's just another way for her to be all show-offy about her tons of money. I bet her real last name is something non-richy-sounding and even totally boring. Like Snuffledorf or Gickerbob. Or Blah.

But definitely not Becker.

Mia Street Claire

BACK TO THE GIRLS' ROOM . . .

Okay, this is what I heard Mia say to Alissa, a seventh grader who's not popular, but not totally unpopular either. Actually, just talking to Mia bumped her up on the popularity scale by 3 points. But she did start talking to Mia first, so -1 point for that.

I have filled in the blanks in the spots where I couldn't actually hear every word, but I'm pretty positive about what was being said:

Alissa: Your hair is so fabulous.

Mia: Isn't it? I love myself so much.

Alissa: So, guess what I heard?

Mia: What?

Alissa: Someone has a crush on you.

Mia: Of course. Doesn't everyone?

I'm totally wonderful. Who is it?

Alissa: Well, I heard Andrew talking

to Josh about you and . . .

WHAT?! Andrew is crushing on Mia St. Claire?

That's where I stopped overhearing. Because at

that exact moment my heart was tragically taken out

of my chest, thrown on the ground, and trampled on

by a thousand elephants into a million tiny pieces.

And then eaten by starving vultures

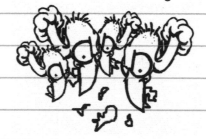

Andrew can't like her! He just can't. Seriously.

Because he likes me, Sofia! Sometimes he calls me

Barfia, but that's just a pet name. Boys can be

dumb like that. They don't know how to show

their true feelings ~~sometimes~~. ~~Most of the time~~.
All of the time.

Hey, Barfia!

 Andrew is not just cute, he is THE cutest guy in
all of sixth grade. He's the class president and he
has a sense of humor that makes me spit chocolate
milk through my nose.

Love Story Randomness

Once Upon a Time . . .

I tried to show Andrew, in a way he could understand, that I totally like him too.

I like you too!!!

I just closed my eyes and gently tossed an apple. At him. It's not my fault I'm a totally awesome sporty chick with a mean throw.

Andrew was really mad, but really, I don't know what the big deal is. It was only a small concussion.

The Happily Ever After is yet to be determined. Sigh.

TUESDAY 02

?? ? BARFIA ? ? ?

My pet name, Barfia, really only happened by accident. I kinda/maybe/sorta barfed in gym class. But I swear, it wasn't even my fault! I have a very fragile and sensitive stomach. And once in a while, I get motion sickness. Even though technically, I wasn't in motion. Unless you count walking.

I guess Andrew didn't fully appreciate the fragile state my stomach was in that day. Especially when I threw up on his new shoes. But that's what shoe stores are for, right?

I've decided the news about Andrew totally

liking Mia St. Claire must be blogged. At once, immediately! Even though my heart totally aches just thinking about it. But honestly, my blog has been a bit boring lately and readership is down. There's no way my blog will become popular if it's not updated with all the most recent overheard stuff. Once my blog becomes popular, I will of course become popular. Muah ha ha ha.

---

1 Reader + kinda boring = Only almost popular

BFF Nona Bows. I can always count on her.

It's really quite genius, actually. Even though I'm completely and anonymously THE Blogtastic Blogger, I can blog about anything and people will read it. Even super-fantastic stuff about my friends and me that most definitely has the potential to bump us way up on the popularity meter.

Okay, so it's a little lame that my blog is on the school's website. And really lame that the school's newspaper advisor, Mr. Anderson, monitors all the blogginess that goes on (no profanity or anything common sense tells you is a bad idea). And it's super-lame that my blog is just one of many on the site. But . . . this gives me even more reason to update my blog with the best juiciness middle school ears can hear. In fact, I could possibly even be the next big celebrity blogger to the stars. Minus celebrity. And stars.

It shouldn't be long before my blog is on its way to almost-popular status. The second I get home tonight—after homework, dinner, and talking to my BFF Nona Bows—I will decide how to best phrase this most juicy gossip.

Practicing a signature to use when I become all famous-like and sign autographs

Sofia   Regular and boring. I take my celebrity status seriously.

Sofia   The "on the go" look, since I will be a very busy celebrity girl.

Sofia   Notice the happy face? Handwriting experts say this means you're a happy person. Which I totally am.

Sofia   All curly and fancy, which means I'm probably rich and fancy myself. Which I plan to be.

       The "scribble" look. According to my dad's handwriting, this could actually spell my name.

POPULARITY METER

 The essence of popularity, like Mia St. Claire, who's been the absolute since preschool and dares you to take her down.

 **Übercool without Trying to Be Popular** — kids like Andrew or Mike Sprat don't even need to try. They're just cool, which translates to übercoolness.

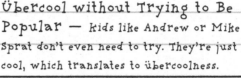 **Kissing Butt to Become Popular** — Those like Penelope, Alyssa, or Megan who try to score popularity points off those who are higher up on the meter than them. AKA popular by association.

 **The Future Populars** — Although we're popularity challenged, we're actually really cool but nobody realizes it yet. We're destined for a future of popularity. We just need to spread the awareness.

 **Never in a Gazillion Years Popular** — Nose pickers, stink bombs, and gross kids are here. Just like Smelly Smelt and Joe (uh) Coolio. Nobody is certain if this is an inherited or learned disability.

248 MINUTES LATER . . .

So with the help of Nona, I've narrowed it down to three possibilities:

1. Andrew has proclaimed his endless crush on Mia St. Claire.

2. Jennifer was seen holding hands with Jeremy Watson.

3. Mia's fakeness and her humongo zit! (Side note: she really has one too! It looked like she grew a second nose. I'm surprised nobody said anything. I bet she'll turn it into a new trend. By tomorrow morning I'll be in a school full of humongo zit noses.)

I'm off now to create a nice little meshed blog paragraph of juiciness. . . .

MIDDLEBROOKE MIDDLE SCHOOL BLOGGER:

BREAKING NEWS FROM THE
BEST BLOG IN THE WORLD. EVER.

Students in the News: M.St.C.'s dark hair of lusciousness is fake. That's right, fake lusciousness! Some people might pay for a haircut, but she just pays for her hair. Maybe the fakeness is to help cover up her jumbo zit which is oh so very real. Also, sixth grader Jen was seen holding hands with seventh grader J.W.

A is madly crushing on M. Perhaps she Googled a spell to put on him?

Teachers in the News: Mr. L's teeth are not real. He lost his real teeth in a terrible accident involving those weird little model trains he collects.

Posted by: The Blogtastic Blogger

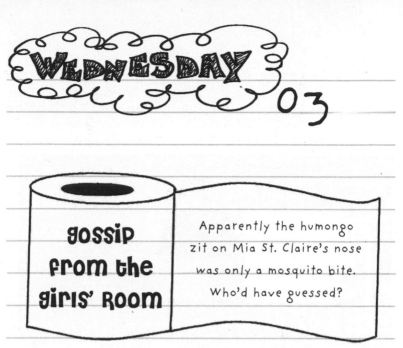

WEDNESDAY 03

gossip from the girls' Room

Apparently the humongo zit on Mia St. Claire's nose was only a mosquito bite. Who'd have guessed?

NOTE TO SELF: Figure out how eighth grader Stanley Sizemore ended up with a face full of mosquito bites.

Contrary to popular opinion (and her last name), Nona Bows is very anti-bow. She might even carry out a Bow Rebellion. And it's not just because Mia St. Claire plasters one to her head every day. It's because Nona and I firmly stand by our belief that bows DO NOT belong on heads. They only belong on wrapped presents and the occasional puppy.

Exceptions of other unwrapped items that may be deemed acceptable with a bow

non-objecting cute giggly babies

ancient old men, like 40 years old

a car for my sixteenth birthday (hint, hint)

I much prefer flowery accessories. Nona can be seen wearing a flower in her hair every single day. Me? Not so much. I'm the kind of girl that likes to admire the prettiness from afar.

TYPES OF NON-WEARING HAIR FLOWERS

dearly departed wilting graveyard flowers

flowers that are disguised to look like flowers but are really weeds

Nona and I are determined to gain newcomer popularity points this year. In addition to my blog, we also decided on a game plan.

Take a super-fun elective class together, and actually talk to the cool kids.

Join an after-school activity that reeks of coolness.

Do whatever we can to get noticed. In a good way, of course, and hopefully get invited to sit at the lunch table for cool kids.

But our game plan hasn't gone exactly as planned. Yet.

Strike 1. We didn't get the same elective class. And mine is definitely not fun.

• Nona got drama (I'm way more dramatic than her!) and I got stuck in stuffy journalism. I like writing, but without all the factual boring stuff.

Strike 2. We joined volleyball as an after-school activity, but *we* don't reek of coolness— only sweat.

My ^Boring Schedule

- Language Arts ← even though there's no drawing involved!

- Geography ← (so non-fun)

- French I ← who, moi? see, I'm basically a pro!

- Math ← 😞 Yuck × 1,000,000,000,000

- Study Hall ♥ ← AKA BLOG TIME!!!

- Elective—Journalism

- Dead Life Science

There are maybe a few bits of greatness about journalism that I, Miss Positive, am trying to look on the bright side about. These bits include:

1. Tables and couches instead of actual regular desks.

2. Ability to speak without raising your hand first.

3. Mobility without having to ask for permission.

4. Mr. Anderson actually encourages us to speak our mind and doesn't send us to detention!

The Miss Negative side of me must keep the balance of the universe by pointing out the Dark Side bits too. Bits such as:

1. The class is run by the editor of the paper, Jimmy, who has an ego the size of Mia's (fake) zit.

2. Mr. Anderson is bent on us learning facts and how to be real reporters, which is B-O-R-I-N-G.

For example, he made us watch the last political debate and take notes the whole time. Then we had to write an article based on it. My paper, titled "Why the Governor Needs a Makeover," was not a part of our mind that he encourages us to speak, apparently.

WEDNESDAY

A LITTLE LATER...

gossip from the girls' Room

Between math and science class, Jane told Rachael that she read about Andrew's crush for Mia St. Claire on some blog. She told her to check it out and I think I heard Rachael nod.

NOTE TO SELF: "Some blog" is me!! Celebrate my utter successfulness for my blog reaching almost-popular status. I checked my stats and . . . get this—it upgraded from one reader to almost a dozen! Hmmm, I wonder if Mia St. Claire was one of them.

Mia St. Claire sat next to Andrew in math class. And they were talking! I pretended not to listen. And even though I was only sort of mildly interested, I dropped my pencil and had to lean waaaay over to pick it up. So I might have heard what they were talking about. And it might have sounded like this:

Andrew: Did you read that blog by the Blogtastic Blogger?

Mia St. Claire: Yes. (Observational note: she throws her head back and laughs even though his sentence was completely non-funny.)

Andrew: That's something, huh?

Mia St. Claire: Yes. (Observational note: once again, she tosses her hair over her shoulder and laughs.)

Andrew: So, you want to study in the library later?

Have my non-wax-filled ears failed me? Why is Andrew asking Mia to study? They never study. It just doesn't make sense. I mean, sure, he has a crush on her and all, but . . .

And on a total side note, I will simply die if he professes his crush for her all wannabe-poetic. So totally cliché and lame. Unless he did that for me.

ON THE
BIKE RIDE HOME
Alone

Nona has already decided that she will become a big-time actress. Someday. So she's trying out for the school play, to get a jump on her career. I would've played the total supportive friend role if the tryouts weren't closed. I don't think her actress days will last long, though. It's like last year when she made cookies for a school fund-raiser and decided she was destined to be a chef.

and that one time last week when she saw an infomercial for makeup and thought she was meant to be a makeup artist

For the first time in forever, I have to bike home from school friendless.

When I get home I barely make it through the front door without tripping on boxes. It looks like we either just moved in or we run a secret box factory out of our living room. But I know better. It's Wednesday. Dad has cleaned out the garage every Wednesday for as long as I can remember. Every Wednesday he goes through only one or two boxes before getting sidetracked. Last week, midway through a box he became sidetracked by the discovery of his old comic book collection. After reading them for several hours, he packed the stuff back up, only to do it all over again the next Wednesday. I think this is just Dad's way to look busy so he doesn't have to do the dishes.

OTHER PREVIOUS SIDETRACKING ITEMS

- Model cars that looked 100 years old (he calls them antiques)
- Key chain collection (because you never know when you'll lose one)
- Old dusty hats (that I could never imagine anyone wearing in public)

I try to sneak upstairs to my room, but it's too late. My dad spots me through the heaps of cardboard and enthusiastically says, "Sofia! Come see what I found!" Which translates to "Come look at my newest rediscovery that will be of no interest to you but I will still talk to you about it for way too long."

This is soooo interesting! Trust me!

Wink, Wink

WHAT FEELS LIKE 54 HOURS LATER BUT IS REALLY ONLY 30 MINUTES

I finally break free of my dad and his old baseball cards from when he was a kid. He says they're worth a lot of money but refuses to sell them. Adults are so unexplainable.

I try concentrating on my homework but my mind keeps wandering to Nona and her tryouts. If she does get the part I hope she doesn't have to spend a lot of time going to play practice and less time hanging out and doing homework with me. To preoccupy my mind with something else, I decide to blog. And although I don't have anything gossipy at precisely the moment, I post the first thing that comes to mind.

MIDDLEBROOKE MIDDLE SCHOOL BLOGGER:

BREAKING NEWS FROM THE

BEST BLOG IN THE WORLD. EVER.

This blog is ridiculously übercool and has all the best and latest info in the school. Just saying.

Posted by: The Blogtastic Blogger

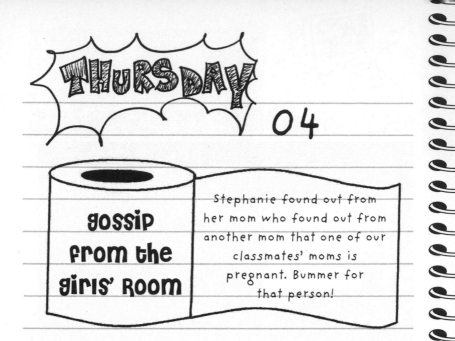

THURSDAY

04

gossip from the girls' Room

Stephanie found out from her mom who found out from another mom that one of our classmates' moms is pregnant. Bummer for that person!

NOTE TO SELF: Find out who the classmate in question is and get all the bloggy details.

Life science class should be called dead science. Dead as in we have to dissect something that was once alive. Mr. Q (his name is something like Quiquejkdsjiouiofadjkfj, which nobody knows how to pronounce. I don't even think he does) assigned us our projects today. Scott Barley, TGBE (The Grossest Boy Ever), was told to hand out the assignment sheets. When he got to my desk, he burped really loud and laughed like it was actually funny or something. I wish I could dissect him so I could figure out why rude kids act that way.

Mr. Q hasn't spilled the beans about what exactly we're dissecting, and I'm in no hurry to find out. All he revealed is that we'll be writing a ten-page report! The only positive is we get to share the grossness with a partner. Nona and I will totally rock as partners! She can take her anger out on whatever poor insect or creature we get, and I'll take notes. Maybe I'll even peek a little too, just so the ewww factor is evenly distributed. As long as we don't have to dissect a parrot. Sam Sam would be crushed knowing I was dissecting one of his relatives.

Grossness
unfunny humor
ACTS RUDE
Bad behavior
mean to Girls
Likes Dirt

what the brain of a rude boy probably looks like

During study hall I'm able to use the school's computer lab to update my blog. Though sometimes it's hard when a kid tries to sit right next to me and be all up in my business. I totally need privacy and nobody seems to get that. Like yesterday, TGBE kept looking at my screen saying, "What are you doing?" over and over again. I nearly renicknamed him The Most Annoying Boy Ever.

Trying to blog at home is a major pain too. My parents always push their nosiness into my room to see what I'm doing. And they make totally ridiculous excuses. Once my mom said she lost an earring and had to search my room for it. She looked in my drawers, under my mattress, and in a box on the top shelf of my closet.

Hmmm, no earring here.

SOFIA'S COMPUTER

and on my computer

At least today in computer lab the seat next to me is kid-free and clear of any oncoming nosiness. I take the chance to update my blog.

MIDDLEBROOKE MIDDLE SCHOOL BLOGGER:

BREAKING NEWS FROM THE

BEST BLOG IN THE WORLD. EVER.

Students in the News: Shannon L. just got a new puppy, and named it Shannon. I wonder how that works. Shannon, it's time to walk Shannon. Sit, Shannon, stay!

Posted by: The Blogtastic Blogger

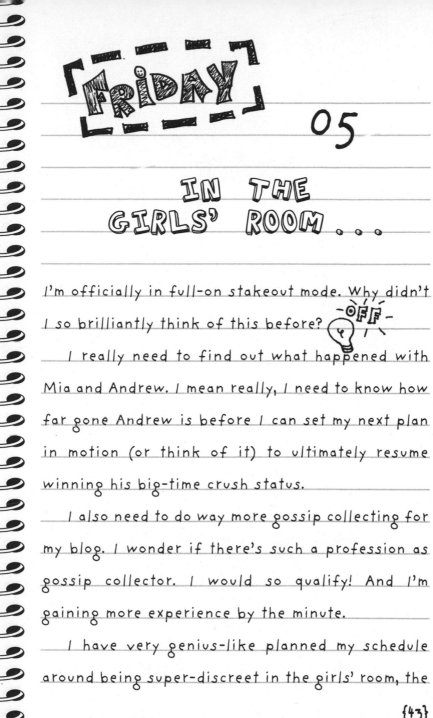

FRIDAY

05

IN THE GIRLS' ROOM...

I'm officially in full-on stakeout mode. Why didn't I so brilliantly think of this before? —OFF—

I really need to find out what happened with Mia and Andrew. I mean really, I need to know how far gone Andrew is before I can set my next plan in motion (or think of it) to ultimately resume winning his big-time crush status.

I also need to do way more gossip collecting for my blog. I wonder if there's such a profession as gossip collector. I would so qualify! And I'm gaining more experience by the minute.

I have very genius-like planned my schedule around being super-discreet in the girls' room, the cafeteria, and other gossip-infested places, every chance I get.

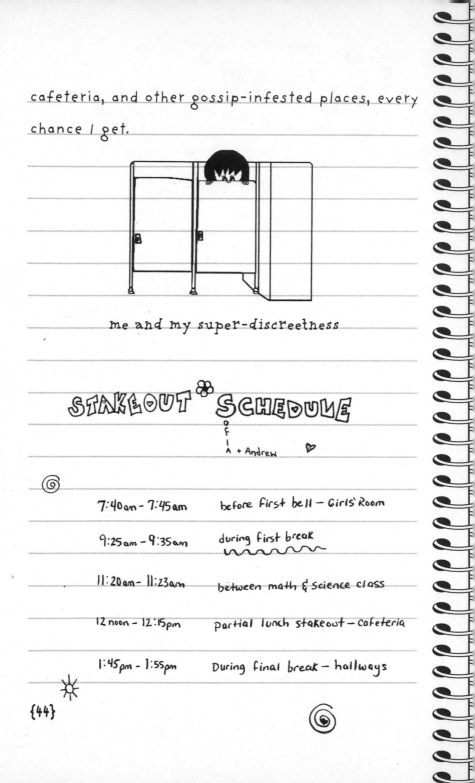

me and my super-discreetness

STAKEOUT ✿ SCHEDULE
o
f
I
A + Andrew ♡

7:40am - 7:45am	before first bell - Girls' Room
9:25am - 9:35am	during first break
11:20am - 11:23am	between math & science class
12 noon - 12:15pm	partial lunch stakeout - cafeteria
1:45pm - 1:55pm	During final break - hallways

So isn't it just my luck that Mia St. Claire happened to be in the girls' room at precisely the exact moment as me? And isn't it just my luck that all the stalls are once again occupied except for the Stink-Haunted one? Okay, so the other girls' room is way on the other side of campus, but still, it's a big coincidence.

Tomorrow come better prepared.

Mia St. Claire was talking to somebody nameless (meaning I could only see the back of her head). And it almost looked like the back of Math Cheater Megan's head. Maybe.

Conversation with most of
the correct facts as I remember them:

Mia St. Claire: I can't believe this!

My brand-new shirt is ruined!

Nameless girl: What happened?

Mia St. Claire: A bird pooped on me!

keeping my reaction to a minimum

I peek through the crack of the stall door to get a better view.

Mia St. Claire was vigorously rubbing her shirt, even though it was clear to us onlookers (me and nameless girl) that the bird poop was not going to come out. In fact, it looked as if she might have to walk around with a poop stain on her shirt. Except, you couldn't tell entirely that it was poop. I mean, maybe she just spilled milk. Or ice cream. Even though it's not lunch yet. But on the bright side, I bet Mia St. Claire totally stinks now! Andrew will HAVE to notice that.

And he will have to notice how nicely I smell compared to her.

Noticeable Observation:
Mia St. Claire is still wearing part of the bird! Nameless girl hasn't even mentioned the feather on her head. I wonder if she's just being blind on purpose.

Has her head sprouted wings?

If Mia even has the slightest idea that
this feather is present on the top of her superbly,
stupendously styled hair, her rich girl
~~expression doesn't show it.~~

Yes, I know! It has come to my attention that
this situation contains definite potential
blogability. Except for the fact that everyone will
see it before it's actually blogged. But that's okay.
I'm sure not EVERYONE will see it. And those that
do will love to hear (read) about it again (myself
included). Nona stands guard while I update on the
computer in the library during lunch.

MIDDLEBROOKE MIDDLE SCHOOL BLOGGER:

BREAKING NEWS FROM THE

BEST BLOG IN THE WORLD. EVER.

Students in the News: Mia St. Claire got into a fight with a bird. And lost. No matter how much she scrubbed her shirt, it was ruined with the leftover white substance that is known as "bird poo." Not to mention, the latest trend of wearing bird feathers has been established by Mia St. Claire.

Parents in the News: Justin Doral's mom was seen in the mall parking lot wearing a very bright neon orange vest and blowing a whistle.

Posted by: The Blogtastic Blogger

Blog Comment by Advisor Mr. A: It's best to not use actual names of students. Gossip might seem fun, but it can hurt those you write about.

I was so super-excited about receiving my first blog comment but totally bummed when I realized it was from Mr. Anderson. And it shouldn't even be called a comment, but a lecture.

Sat + Sun

06 & 07

Weekends smoosh together, like one big meshed day of non-schooling. It should be called something like Sunturday. Like someone threw Saturday and Sunday into a boiling pot of water, then mashed them into a thick lumpy batter. I'm always thinking Saturday is Sunday and Sunday is Saturday so if it's Sunturday, I could never be wrong.

Nona declared today National Bird-Watching Day on behalf of Mia St. Claire's "bird incident." But then my mom told us that there really is such a day and we checked the calendar but didn't see it. I guess it's one of those fake kind of holidays that people probably make up just to sound super-important. Which leads me to really give deep consideration to the fact that I should have a day or month named after me. Like National Super-Cool Sofia Month or something. Talk about winning popularity points there!

I wonder if I could just declare it and then it's official, or if I have to get a patent or trademark or something. I better be careful and not blog about this since Mia St. Claire would probably steal this idea and with all of her money, she'd end up buying a year and not just a month in her name. Like National Mia St. Claire Gorgeousness Year. Oh well, I have all weekend to think about it.

Me and Nona played our Would You Rather? game. You take turns giving each other two choices and you have to truthfully tell which one you'd rather do.

Nona: Would you rather stick a pencil
in your eye or shave your head?
Me: Shave my head. I'd rather wear a
wig than an eye patch.

Nona: Would you rather kiss your parrot or kiss your mom in public?

Me: Parrot. Definitely.

Nona: Would you rather eat shelled peanuts or lick a metal pole in a snowstorm?

Me: Easy, peanuts.

Then it was my turn.

Me: Would you rather eat mud that tasted like chocolate or chocolate that tasted like mud?

Nona: Pie.

Me: That wasn't even an option!

Nona: I don't like mud or chocolate. So I chose pie.

I hate when Nona changes the rules to games while we're playing them.

Another instance when Nona changed a rule

I found you!

Nope! I'm invisible now.

Hide-and-Seek

Nona tries to act all genius-like by telling me I should blog about myself. I told her the plan is once the blog is cool then I will write about how cool we are too. She says no, I need to write about my "uncool self." Although that totally defeats the purpose of my blog. Why in the galaxy would I want to do that?

Nona's theory is this: If THE Blogtastic Blogger WASN'T me, then the embarrassing or stupid stuff that happens to me would be blogged about. So by me keeping myself exempted from such happenings, in a way, I'm announcing my identity.

I told her this makes a little sense.

I make a mental note to secretly track my dumb happenings, instead of pushing them to the very back of my brain and dumping them into the pit of forgetfulness to cover up such unpopular tragedies and protect me from being traumatized for the rest of my life.

HISTORY OF UNPOPULAR MIDDLE-SCHOOL TRAGEDIES

Eighth-grade bully Jeremy got his braces stuck to the sweater of a sixth grader.

Seventh grader Anastasia had gum stuck in her hair and had to shave half her head.

Sixth grader Noah fell asleep while making a Mother's Day card. He went the whole day not realizing he had the word "mom" printed across his forehead.

MONDAY

08

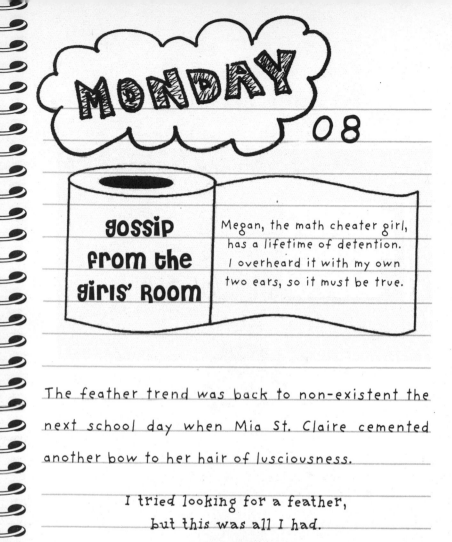

gossip from the girls' Room

Megan, the math cheater girl, has a lifetime of detention. I overheard it with my own two ears, so it must be true.

The feather trend was back to non-existent the next school day when Mia St. Claire cemented another bow to her hair of lusciousness.

I tried looking for a feather,
but this was all I had.

As much as I hate to admit it (about as much as I hate broccoli—which is a lot!), Mia St. Claire and I, Sofia Becker, are actually, in fact, very similar.

SIMILARITIES INCLUDED BUT NOT LIMITED TO:

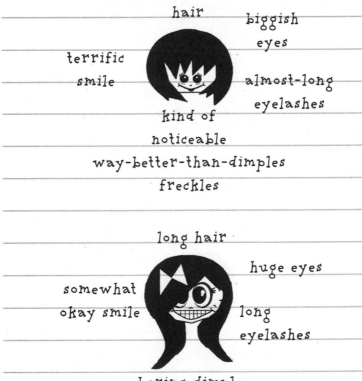

hair

biggish eyes

terrific smile

almost-long eyelashes

kind of

noticeable

way-better-than-dimples

freckles

long hair

huge eyes

somewhat okay smile

long eyelashes

boring dimple

ANOTHER TOTAL SIMILARITY

Her name ends in -ia. So does mine. Which in all reality, makes me only a +M —Sof away from being a Mia.

SIMILARITY EXCEPTIONS

Ridiculous hair feathers

snobbish attitude
(hers, not mine)

noticeable
snobbishness

Cute, trainable
parrot Sam Sam
(Mine, not hers. I
know she's jealous!)

—Mia stinks!

Mia and Andrew update: Andrew spotted at Mia's locker holding her books. I could just almost quite possibly die!

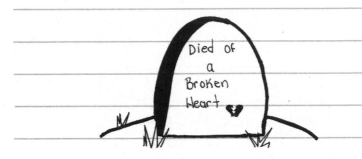

Here lies Sofia Becker.
Such a sad, sad tragedy.

I shove my cell phone into my locker before first period, refusing to think about them. Nona gives me a weird look and I'm suddenly aware she's eyeballing my phone. And then she asks me since when did I get a cell phone?

I try to act like it's no big deal because I know how badly Nona wants one.

what? This old thing?

I also don't tell her that despite a bazillion months of begging Mom for the phone, she finally only gave in because I started riding my bike to school this year. Even though I only live two blocks away, my mom is super-paranoid. She probably even has a tracking device on my bike wheels.

And even though Nona is probably obsessing over how my mom is ultimately way cooler than hers, she acts like she doesn't care. And I act like I don't care that she doesn't care. And even more, having a cell phone isn't THAT awesome because of all the rules. And I won't admit this to any non-cell phone owners since it does make me seem a tiny bit cooler.

What's funny (not haha funny but more like stupid funny) is that I suspect that the parents and the school had a secret meeting to make similar rules to ruin our lives.

Parents' Rules for Cell Phones:

- Can only use minutes with permission.
- Cannot text during school hours.
- Parents can snoop at any time.

Similarly Scary School Rules for Cell Phone:

- Must keep phone in locker during class.

- Cannot text during school hours.
- School can confiscate phones (and snoop) any time rules are not followed.

It's hard enough to remember all the rules for home, how are we expected to remember the hundreds of rules for school?

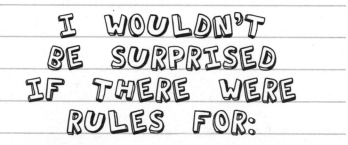

I WOULDN'T BE SURPRISED IF THERE WERE RULES FOR:

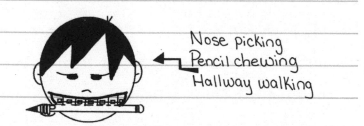

Nose picking
Pencil chewing
Hallway walking

THE BUZZ AROUND SCHOOL . . .

People are actually reading my blog. MY blog! I almost feel like a superhero. THE Blogtastic Blogger—making the world (aka Middlebrooke Middle School) a little more entertaining, one post at a time.

I feel so powerful to be able to write about anything and others will read it. And talk about it. Now I just need to make sure I keep blogging posts with crazy juiciness so my readers will keep coming back for more. In no time I'll have enough readers to be able to blog great things about my friends and me. And I could quite possibly become popular. But I refuse to wear a bow.

People are wondering which classmate has the pregnant mom. From what I heard (while accidentally dropping my pen by the office while Amelia was talking to Emma) it's a girl. I think it's kinda cool. It would be like being able to babysit. Only full-time! Uh, and not getting paid. Never mind.

I'm an only child but Nona has always been like a sister to me. We've known each other from the uncomfortable days of being cramped up in our mothers' stomachs. Our moms are BFFs, which made us destined to be BFFs too. They said we were already trying to kick our way out every time they were in the same room. I think in all reality that was more of Nona being claustrophobic and me probably having gas.

Apparently Mom loved eating Mexican food when I was in her belly.

TUESDAY 09

RANDOM OBSERVATION

Sometimes, I have this problem with my brain. It has the tendency to go numb at the worst moments. It's like getting brain freeze, without the pain.

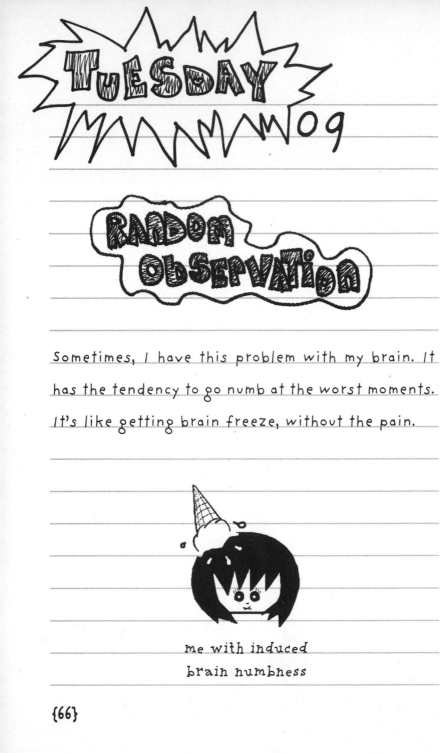

me with induced
brain numbness

Maybe it's contagious, because today Nona took out her backpack during geography, and forgot why.

Or that could have also been brought on due to Zombiness.

Zombiness (zom-bee-ness), noun: something that happens during Mr. Allen's geography class brought on by complete and utter boringness.

the zombie side of me

Today, Mr. Allen asked us each to share which state we chose for our State Report. My response? Zombiness. I wasn't paying attention, and when he asked in a not-very-friendly voice, "Sofia? Your state?" all I could say was, "Um . . . confusion?" He was very unhappy with me. He probably would've sent me to the principal's office had he not secretly known it was his fault for causing the Zombiness in the first place. Even my own father would side with me.

I totally believe Mr. Allen induced Zombiness and it's not your fault you're unable to pay attention. Mr. Allen deserves to go to the principal's office, not my most perfect daughter, Sofia Becker.

Mia St. Claire, in all of her politeness, raised her hand and asked to use the lavatory.

UM, THE WHAT?

As soon as she left the classroom, I asked to use the girls' room. But really, with my quick-on-my-feet smartness, I had a plan.

I, Sherlock Sofia, will solve the mystery of the "lavatory" in question, by using my super-stealth quickness and following Mia St. Claire. Unknowingly.

the mysterious lavatory mystery

What could it be? It sounds like maybe a super-secret laboratory. But why would Middlebrooke Middle School have a super-secret lab? And why would Mia need to go there?

2 MINUTES, 24 SECONDS LATER . . .

My days (minutes?) of Sherlock Sofia were not very long-lived. Sigh.

I followed Mia St. Claire straight to the girls' room.

Who knew—besides Mia St. Claire—that "lavatory" is just a fancy way of saying bathroom? The words don't even sound the least bit similar. I bet she invented that word because really, bathrooms are so totally the opposite of fancy.

Come to think of it, Mia St. Claire DOES write with a pen that is full of fanciness. I wonder what she calls that . . .

a penatory?

THE HISTORY OF MAKING UP NAMES

Sam Sam—His name was Sam, but he likes to repeat words a lot, so he kind of renamed himself.

Sofia—My mom couldn't come up with a name. But then she sat on a sofa . . . bingo! Inspiration! But since Sofa doesn't sound very girly, my parents added the letter "I," which makes anything sound more girly.

Nona—I'm not sure how her parents came up with it. She won't even tell me her middle name And I've known her forever! I'm pretty sure her parents were hippies. So they probably named her after a tree they hugged. Or maybe her mom didn't have any inspiration like mine and Nona stands for No Name.

Mia—She's all about me, me, me. So her name is perfect.

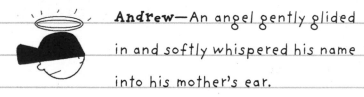

Andrew—An angel gently glided in and softly whispered his name into his mother's ear.

MIDDLEBROOKE MIDDLE SCHOOL BLOGGER:

BREAKING NEWS FROM THE
BEST BLOG IN THE WORLD. EVER.

Students in the News: E.S.'s older brother got warts from touching a frog. Maybe E will catch warts now too?

Teachers in the News: Mrs. T brings leftover cafeteria food home for dinner every night because she doesn't know how to cook. She even burns water in the microwave.

Posted by: The Blogtastic Blogger

WEDNESDAY

10

Dead science class stinks! And not just because of the rotting bugs that Mr. Q keeps in a desk drawer (long story).

We were randomly and unwillingly paired up for our project. I'm not sure why, but Mr. Q is out to get me. I'm paired up with Miss Snooty Pants, Penelope, aka Mia wannabe. Actually, she's more like Mia's sidekick. She's way meaner than Mia. She's like a panda, really. Looks all sweet and innocent, but is totally vicious I learned from a documentary that pandas attack when irritated. And really, when does Penelope NOT seem irritated?

Penelope's reaction when it was announced we'd be partners

looks painful, right?

I glanced at Nona, knowing her look of misery would make me feel that much better now that I was stuck with Penelope. But, horribly, it had the opposite effect. She doesn't seem one bit miserable that we're not partners. In fact, she looks so happy, it's like she barely remembers I exist. All because she's partnered with Joey. The runner-up to the cutest boy in school ever. Deep down, I know Nona wishes I were her partner instead. Deep down, I know that drama class is affecting her behavior and she's becoming a good actress. And she totally deserves an Academy Award for this performance.

Because deep down, I know no girl should ever be this happily gushing over a guy. Unless the guy is Andrew. And the girl is me.

The stages of your BFF crushing on a guy:

Stage 1. She notices the guy noticing her.

Stage 2. Spending more time with guy and way less time with BFF.

Stage 3. Denial about spending less time with BFF.

Stage 4. BFF is dumped for guy like yesterday's garbage.

THURSDAY

11

LOST!

Mega Mini Crisis! My Pre-Blogging Notebook was lost! As in, someone probably stole it.

Fortunately I recovered it in the girls' room on my latest stakeout. It was on the floor of the Stink-Haunted Stall. (I know, gross!!) And it was out of my possession for approximately 15 hours, 26 minutes, and 3.5 seconds.

But here's the bad news that makes my heart drop heavily to my feet at 100 miles per hour, like some winding speeding roller coaster that falls off the edge of the track at precisely the most unexpected moment.

There is a footprint on MY notebook.

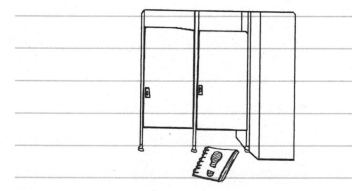

This means:

Somebody other than myself has been in the Stink-Haunted Stall, and somebody stepped on my notebook!

Possibly somebody READ my notebook.

Somebody has a really big foot!

I can't help but wonder (and panic!) if someone did in fact read this super-secret notebook disguised as a regular and very ordinary-looking notebook. I plan to find out ASAP. I'm sure I'll hear some talk of it around school if that did happen.

But until then it's like I can't think of anything else at this precise exact moment. Even Mr. Anderson noticed and asked me what was wrong during journalism. It's not like I could possibly tell him my entire life may very well be flushed down the toilet. How in the world could he ever understand?

Teachers have a way of knowing when

things are wrong with their students

Hmm, my super-
sensitive teacher sense
detects a problem.

86-1/2 MINUTES LATER...

Okay, so I have creatively collaborated with

Nona, who very intelligently told me we must do

something to distract me from the possibility that

my notebook was invaded.

Nona also made me assure her that I stuck to the Friendship Pact.

That's where Nona promised to never tell anyone that my super-secret notebook existed, and I promised to never say anything bad about Nona in my notebook. Even if we're fighting and I totally want to vent my feelings of anger.

We even did a blood pact to prove our seriousness. Except, blood really freaks me out. So does the color red. So we used mustard.

All my notebook stressfulness makes me lose track of time and I'm almost late to Ms. Peabody's math class. She is verrrry strict and usually locks the door the second the bell stops ringing to get her point across that tardiness is non-acceptable.

Peabody is a very appropriate name for her, since her body kind of looks like peas. The kind you spit out in your napkin and hide under your plate at dinner. But like 80 times that size.

Non-acceptable!

AFTER SCHOOL

Nona helped me realize—actually she nodded while I did all the realizing—that a blog about something totally un-notebook-related could help to throw everyone off my track. Or at least give everyone something else to talk about, just in case.

realization nodding in action

my "I'm totally realizing" face

MIDDLEBROOKE MIDDLE SCHOOL BLOGGER:

BREAKING NEWS FROM THE

BEST BLOG IN THE WORLD. EVER.

Students in the News: M will begin her lifetime sentence of detention for cheating on the very all-important math exam. She wrote the answers on the bottom of her shoe, but she wrote so tiny, her eyeballs were practically glued to her shoe trying to read it. How could anyone NOT know she was cheating?

Teachers in the News: Mrs. B is getting braces! Now she'll look just like her students.

Posted by: The Blogtastic Blogger

Blog Comment by Anon Student 1: Bummer on the detention thing.

{83}

Blog Comment by Anon Student 2: I asked Mrs. B and she said that is just a rumor.

Blog Comment by Anon Student 3: The person who cheated should have written the answers on her hand instead.

Blog Comment by Advisor Mr. A: Cheating is very serious and the teachers will have a conference with your parents if this happens. Please think twice before doing this.

Blog Comment by Anon Student 3: I wasn't saying she should have cheated, I just meant she was dumb about it.

FRIDAY

IN THE GIRLS' ROOM...

Mia sashays in while I'm the only other person in the girls' room—and not in the Stink-Haunted Stall this time. Yay! As she's washing her hands, Penelope click-clacks in with her new expensive-looking shoes that Mia St. Claire immediately takes notice of.

Girls like Mia St. Claire are immediately drawn to expensive things the way a monkey is instantly drawn to a banana.

So after Mia and Penelope stop yapping about the shoes, Mia asks Penelope if anyone else is in the girls' room. I hop up on the toilet seat and crouch down. Sure enough, Penelope peeps under each stall quickly to see if any shoes (probably less expensive than hers) are noticeably visible in the bathroom.

Thinking the coast is clear, Mia lets one fly. No, not THAT. The gossip.

Mia St. Claire: Do you think Mike likes me?

Penelope: Doesn't that one girl like him? (-1 popularity point)

Mia St. Claire: Really? I haven't noticed.

Well, does <u>he</u> like her?

Penelope: Of course not. He likes you. Who doesn't?

Mia St. Claire: Promise not to say a word to anyone?

Penelope: Definitely! (+1 popularity point)

Whoa, wait just a minute there, expensive shoe admirer! Mike? Nona's biggest crush since (last month) nearly almost forever?

I didn't notice that one girl liked him.

Somehow Mia St. Claire can make a
pants-on-fire tragedy look like cheerleading.

I can hear Mia St. Claire smiling gigantically and flashing her overly white teeth, even though there are no boys in her presence. I think she must save those enormously fake smiles for special occasions. Such as secret-keeping occasions like this, for example.

Obviously satisfied, she goes back to talking about Penelope's shoes. Rich people can be so boring!

I get a cramp in one of my crouching legs but luckily the bell rings in time to drown out my screams.

Now I totally find myself in such a horrible predicament. Do I tell Nona about this latest development? Or do I act like the BFF I am and patiently wait this out until I get more facts? I mean, there's probably like a trillion guys named Mike at Middlebrooke Middle School. So maybe I shouldn't jump to any conclusions. After all, gossip is a horrible thing to spread. . . .

IN ZOMBIE CLASS...

I'm totally enveloped in my thoughts and have fallen victim to another case of Zombiness. I jump when I hear Mr. Allen smack his ruler unnecessarily against his desk. When I look up, he's giving me the evil eye. Then, to make his point about how unhappy he is with me, he makes me go to the front of the room and point out different countries on the world map.

When I sit back down, I hear laughter. Not like the loud haha laughter, but the quiet whisper giggling that comes from the back of the room and rolls to the front like a huge wave crashing to the shore. Except I'm the shore (or maybe a fish the sea rejected) because the laughter rolls right over me and I'm totally not getting the funny part.

Nona pokes me in the back with her pencil (the sharp end) and leans forward to tell me I have something on my shoe. I look down and when I see it, my face turns bright red. I know this because every time my face turns red, I start feeling horribly hot. Like my head is blazing. Like a pot of boiling potatoes.

Mrs. Potato Head?

Stuck to the bottom of my sneaker is toilet paper about a mile long. Everyone saw this when I walked to the front of the class. But even more horrific, Penelope jabs me in my right side with her pen (cap end), which she never does because she's too cool to poke uncool people like me. So my stunned self looks toward her and it seems as if everything is in slow motion when she says, "Were you just in the bathroom?"

{90}

I can't say I was in the girls' room since she did a shoe check and would know I was hiding if I was there. And sixth graders never use the girls' room on the other side of campus. It's an unwritten rule that those are only for seventh and eighth graders. But I can't deny the fact that I have toilet paper stuck to my shoe either.

My brain goes numb once again as I try so very desperately to think of what to say on the spur of the moment. But my very detailed eyes come to my rescue as I spot something on Penelope's shoe. So instead of answering, I point.

Just like me, she has toilet paper stuck to the bottom of her shoe. But on the disappointing side, it's only a few squares long. And nobody but me saw. But it was at least enough to make her turn around and forget that I didn't answer her question.

Or did she?

There was way too much tp stuck to my shoe
to have unraveled just a roll. It was more
like I unraveled a mummy.

MIDDLEBROOKE MIDDLE SCHOOL BLOGGER:

BREAKING NEWS FROM THE

BEST BLOG IN THE WORLD. EVER.

Students in the News: M.St.C. is now crushing on M. This is most probably the same exact M. that N.B. is crushing on but has been too shy to admit it to anyone. N.B. may be challenging M.St.C. to a fight after school. Stay tuned for more details.

P's new shoes, although expensive and shiny-looking, are really imposters. Yep, you heard it here first. P's brand names are all knockoffs. Who does she think she's fooling?

Posted by: The Blogtastic Blogger

Blog Comment by Anon Student 1: *I'd like to see that fight.*

Blog Comment by Anon Student 2: My bet is on N.B. . . . Nona Bows, right?

Blog Comment by Advisor Mr. A: Fighting is strictly against school rules. Refrain from blogging about acts of violence.

SUNTUPDAY

13 & 14

Nona heard the rumor that she was supposed to fight Mia. She asked if I knew anything about it. I fessed up and told her I blogged it about because it made the post sound more interesting. Until Mr. Anderson commented. Leave it to him to turn something I casually blog about into an opportunity to enforce a school rule.

Although slightly mad, Nona forgave me and asked me not to blog about her again. She's only slightly mad because she doesn't know about the crush part. But how can I tell her that I blogged about her crush? I mean, I only posted that because I wanted to rat Mia out so Andrew would see that she likes someone else too and I wanted Mike to know (if he reads the blog) that Mia is the wrong girl to like. He should like Nona instead.

So, I did what I could to distract Nona AWAY from my blog during the weekend. Luckily she was out shopping with her mom most of Saturday. Sunday she's coming over for our usual game night, so I'll just make sure not to talk about my blog.

I never thought I'd try to get one of my most loyal readers to NOT read my blog. But desperate times call for drastic measures. Nona would be heartbroken if she read it and found out the truth about Mike. And really, being the bestest friend ever that I am to her, I will do whatever I can to make sure her heart does not get broken like mine. Well, until we can find a way to take Mia St. Claire down. And by then she shouldn't care that I blogged about her one last time.

Question: Could my weekend get any way worse?
Answer: YES.

AT HOME...

My dad had a sit-down talk with me, Sofia Becker, his most favorite (and only) daughter. A sit-down talk usually indicates a much more serious talk than a stand-up talk. He said he needed to remind me that *I* should always support my mother with her career. Which in dad language translates to "your mom is doing something you're not going to like, but live with it."

My mom is a substitute teacher. She subs at other middle schools. Not mine. Any school but mine. That's the unspoken agreement we've had for my entire life.

NEVER EVER EVER EVER EVER EVER EVER sub at my school. Ever.

I can't wait to work at Sofia's school! In fact I'll do everything I can to sub there ASAP!

So now I'm actually getting that happy little butterfly dancing feeling in my stomach. Is Mom getting a new job? A job far away from any school I may ever be at? Mom walks into the room with that happy smiley look on her face that matches my butterfly stomach dance feeling and yes, I think she's about to break the news that she is going to become . . . a hairstylist! Or a fashion magazine writer! Or . . .

I'm subbing at your school!

All my not-quite-worse days have officially come to a screeching halt. And those happy little dancing butterflies? Have died. A very quick and painful death.

MY very own mother is subbing at MY school. How could she do this to me? I could so die of embarrassment. Mom explains that she is placed wherever she is needed, and she just happens to be needed at my school.

Died of Humiliation (total)

Here lies Sofia. Another great tragedy.

Dad, who totally gets me, plastered a fake smile on his face and nodded, trying to prompt me to flash an equally fake smile.

I should've looked like this

But instead I looked like I
swallowed my cell phone

Nokia flip phone with
unlimited texts stuck
in my precious esophagus

HERE'S THE DEAL....

My mom is very loud. And when she's in teacher
mode? Forget it.

But now with her in my school and wandering
aimlessly through the halls and basically out in
public among my social peers, her loudness will be
totally unavoidable. And embarrassing.

In first grade my mom brought cupcakes to my class on my birthday. But really, I should've handed out earplugs instead. I believe this to be a very traumatic experience for any child.

OTHER THINGS TO DROWN OUT MOM LOUDNESS

Drowning. Mom would still be loud, but at least I'd be in a better mood.

Mia St. Claire's hand ← Like I would drown myself!

Bananas in eardrums. Almost pleasantly oblivious.

Paper bag over my precious head. While listening to music on my iPod. But not that heavy metal music where it's just like screaming and not music because that would defeat the whole purpose.

I really wasn't in the mood for game night anymore. I would much rather sit sulking in my room. I told Nona not to come over, but she did anyway. And she brought a gallon of chocolate ice cream.

Then we played a lightning round of Would You Rather?

Me: Lick your feet or smell your grandpa's?

Nona: Mine.

Me: Eat a bug or get kicked in the head by a bag lady?

Nona: Bag lady. I could take her.

Me: Have Joey as your science partner or me?

Nona: That's not a yuck question.

Me: It's a Would You Rather? question.

Nona: Let's play Truth or Dare. I pick dare.

And just like that, the subject was changed and Nona was saying tongue twisters with 15 jumbo-size marshmallows wedged into her mouth.

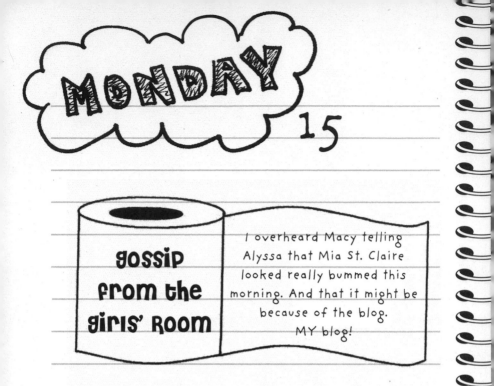

MONDAY 15

gossip from the girls' room

I overheard Macy telling Alyssa that Mia St. Claire looked really bummed this morning. And that it might be because of the blog.
MY blog!

NOTE TO SELF: Check blog stats to see if my readership has doubled. Maybe quadrupled. Or even thousandupled! (It doesn't matter if that's a real word. I can still use it. It's MY notebook.)

So maybe by me acting all sly and cutely unaware, no one will ever think for a moment that my mom is related to me.

SOFIA! My daughter!

HELLOO! Hi, my wonderful daughter Sofia! It's me, your teacher mom ♡

How unlucky am I? I heard someone telling someone else that they heard from someone that MY MOM is subbing at Middlebrooke Middle School. Then I heard accompanying laughter.

Then I heard accompanying crying.

That was from me.

Lucky me. Seriously! Mom is subbing for the first-year Spanish class, since Señor Garcia is apparently sick. And the lucky part is that I don't have this class! But having Teacher Mom sub this class, in all actuality, is really quite funny for one very particular reason. Her extent of Spanish is practically non-existent! In fact, I probably know way more Spanish than her!

Mia Stinko!
squawk!

Jennifer Lopez!
¡Yo quiero Taco Bell!
Chihuahua!
UNO!

This is also very unfunny at the same time because a ton of popular kids are in that class. Which of course evidently means that EVERYONE will know about Mom's Spanish impairment, which only further humiliates me. Thanks, Teacher Mom!

I'm just hoping that Teacher Mom will confine herself exclusively to that classroom to limit my embarrassment potential in the hallways.

THE MANY TYPES OF MOM EMBARRASSMENT

Total   Complete   Utter

Horrible   Stupendous   Obvious

IN DEAD SCIENCE CLASS...

Mr. Q tells us we should exchange email addresses with our partners because we will be spending a lot of homework time writing up our reports. I'd rather clip my grandmother's crusty old toenails than study with Penelope.

While Penelope shuffles off to the teacher's desk to ask a question, Jimmy walks past me and knocks my book off the table. I bend down to pick the book up and I notice it's so very conveniently lying close to Penelope's backpack. And then my brain begins to wonder what girls like Penelope keep in their backpack.

I wouldn't be surprised if Penelope was hiding in her backpack:

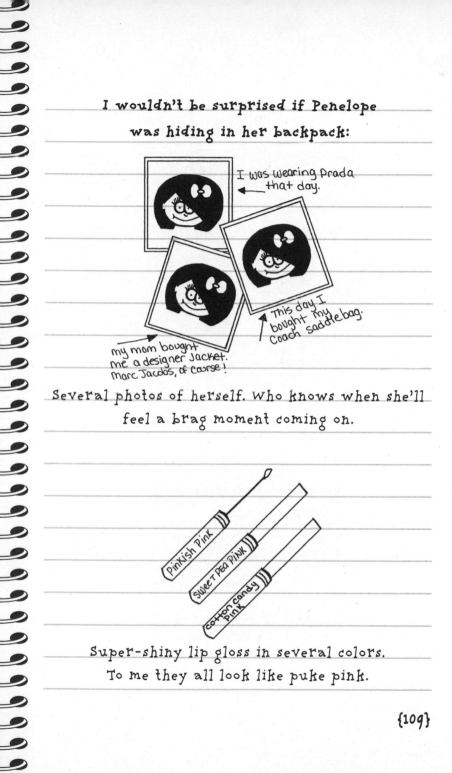

I was wearing Prada that day.

This day I bought my Coach saddle bag.

my mom bought me a designer jacket. Marc Jacobs, of coarse!

Several photos of herself. Who knows when she'll feel a brag moment coming on.

Pinkish Pink

Sweet Pea Pink

Cotton candy pink

Super-shiny lip gloss in several colors. To me they all look like puke pink.

A secret pink diary (notebooks are way better, btw) complete with boy gushing and backstabbing.

My heart thumps like a bongo drum in my ears as I so very quickly rummage through Penelope's backpack, which very disappointedly looks average, and a lot like mine.

Then I see a foot inches from my hand. A foot in a fancy shoe.

"My book fell," I say to Penelope as I sit back in my seat.

"Only guilty people say what they're doing," she says so matter-of-factly. She probably knows firsthand.

So I do the one thing I'm so very talented at doing. I change the subject and ask her for her email.

"You know, so we can . . . study." I almost fake choke on that last word.

She rolls her eyes. But she takes the bait.

"No," she says. "We'll exchange cell numbers. My mom is too nosy and I don't check my email much."

She scribbles her number (probably a fake one!) on a piece of scrap paper that I shove into my backpack and forget about. Then she writes down my number—on her hand, which she will most likely very conveniently wash.

TUESDAY 16

SO STRANGE...

It was the weirdest thing ever. I accidentally forgot how to run laps, due to my sudden concentration on hatching a plan to get back at Mia. Mr. Jim, the smelly gym teacher who has a perspiration problem to boot, took my forgetfulness as lack of participation and sent me to the locker room.

Running?
What's that?

. I'm not sure what Mr. Jim expects me to do in the locker room anyway. Is it like a form of time-out? And if so, can I get it every day? I don't even bother to change out of my non-smelly-never-been-sweaty gym clothes yet. Instead, I sneakily head over to the boys' locker room next door. I've always been curious about what it's like in there. And maybe I will be lucky enough to overhear some boy gossip.

I cannot get caught. I cannot get caught. Ever hear that if you think something really hard it helps to make it come true? Neither have I. But I figured I could try.

No school on weekdays.

Veggies taste like chocolate.

I can turn into a ~~vampire~~ mermaid.

other things I should try to think really hard about

The locker room is dead quiet. And it smells like something dead too. Wow, why do boys smell so bad? In our locker room, it smells like fruity spritzy sprays and floral fragrances. At least we make an effort to mask our stink.

Since the room is boring and unoccupied, I sneak back out before anyone ever knows I was there.

To pass time in the girls' locker room, I take out my notebook and make a list of other blogs on the school website. Since you can view how many people go to each blog, I know exactly which ones I'm in competition with. Most of them are by anonymous students like me. The good news is not many of them blog all the time. Or they just aren't interesting. Like one person posts unfun, non-rhyming poetry that you can't even understand. Another blog has pictures of vintage cars that is updated once a month. But the blogs that should come with a guarantee to cure insomnia include:

Sports talk

Math tips

Weather (we can look outside to

see if it's raining!)

Fishing

But the blogs that are seemingly cool and are probably written by students wanting to be cool, like me, are:

Fashion news for geeks (there are

a lot of us geeks out there!)

Lunch news: the latest on the not-

so greatest

Movie reviews: the newest movies

honestly reviewed

While deep in thought I hear a familiar screaming voice from behind me.

"Sofia!"

HI, HONEY!!!

Why is my mom here in the locker room with me?

"I hear you aren't participating in class?" She sounds all concerned, but that's just one of the ways moms talk to trick you into telling the truth.

"Um, how did you hear that?" Really, how did she? I've only been in gym for twenty minutes.

"Your gym teacher called me in the teachers' lounge since I have this period free. He said you might be sick."

And that's how teachers talk, to get you into trouble with your parents without obviously stating it.

"No, I'm fine. Really."

And as most moms do, she wouldn't take my word

for it. She wanted my temperature taken and dragged me straight to the nurse's office.

MIDDLEBROOKE MIDDLE SCHOOL BLOGGER:

BREAKING NEWS FROM THE

BEST BLOG IN THE WORLD. EVER.

Students in the News: A.S.'s house is haunted. And he sleeps in a coffin.

Teachers in the News: Apparently teachers gossip too.

Blog Comment by Anon Student 1: How do you know this stuff about teachers? Do your parents work here or something?

PROJECT COW EYEBALL

Mr. Q tells us that tomorrow we'll be dissecting cow eyeballs. Real ones! The news produces many different reactions (and sounds) from the class:

Me: Ewww . . . poor cow!

Nona: Cool! Eye juice!

Penelope: Yuck. It better not get on my outfit.

Joey: Awesome! Can we keep them?

Smart kid in the very front row: Will the cornea be intact?

the boy in the front of the class
(nobody knows his name)

Maybe I'll be sick tomorrow and be forced to stay home (cough, cough).

AFTER CLASS...

I hear hushed whispers in the hallway that sound almost identical to the hushed whispers of gossip. It seems to be coming from three lockers down, so I keep busy at my locker doing absolutely nothing but making sure it looks like I'm doing very much of something. Until my mom spots me and waves, yelling my name so loudly that it makes everyone turn to look at me.

I swear her whole point of being at my school is to embarrass me. I stuff my face in my locker, wishing I could crawl inside. Luckily, I can still hear the gossip:

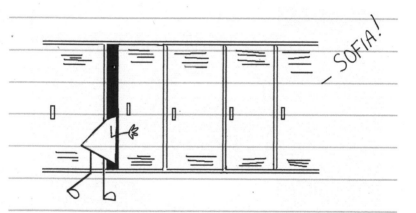

even though it sounds like gossip in a tin can

Stephanie: So do you know which girl's mom is pregnant?

Madison: *No (laughs), but her life will be totally ruined.*

Stephanie: *Tell me about it. When my sister was born it was like I didn't even exist anymore!*

Madison: *I have two older brothers and they are such a pain! I feel sorry for the girl.*

Stephanie: *I know! And how embarrassing to have a mom who's probably totally old being all big and pregnant.*

I didn't find out her identity yet, but I'm sure having a sibling isn't that bad. I mean, Nona and me are practically around each other 24/7. And she does borrow my things without asking. And rats me out to save her own butt. But I maybe kinda might do that too. Sometimes.

But it's not like we ruin each other's lives. Maybe on account of us having different parents who spoil us makes it easier?

Okay, so maybe it's not exactly the same, but I can kind of imagine what it would be like to have a brother or sister.

Nona meets me at my locker and we head to the girls' room so she can do a stakeout with me. It's not crowded, but a girl named Ruby occupies one sink. We pretend to tie our shoes, giving us something to do.

I was wearing sandals,
so I pretended to tie Nona's shoes too.

Then we hear an "eek" from Ruby.

"The sink is clogged!"

She looks at us like we're plumbers or something. The sink is filled to the top with soapy bubbles. Geez, how dirty were Ruby's hands?

She leaves quickly, without even drying her hands, like she's trying to make a getaway. She doesn't even turn the sink completely off.

At precisely that moment, Penelope and Mia walk in. They look from us, to the sink, then back to us. Penelope says, "OMG, what did you guys do?" as water starts to pour over the sides onto the floor.

"We didn't do this," Nona tells her, but of course Penelope rolls her eyes and Mia smirks. Great.

And then even worse? When we all leave the girls' room, my mom just happens to be walking by. And Penelope waves to her and says all sweetly, "Hi, Mrs. Becker. Have you seen the janitor? Sofia flooded the sink."

I could so die.

MIDDLEBROOKE MIDDLE SCHOOL BLOGGER:

BREAKING NEWS FROM THE

BEST BLOG IN THE WORLD. EVER.

Students in the News: R.T. flooded the sink in the girls' room today. Not sure how she did it, but she was seen fleeing from the scene.

Blog Comment from Anon Student 1: What are you talking about? Everyone knows it was Sofia and Nona.

THURSDAY

18

DEAD COW EYEBALL DAY

I wonder who has the totally unfun job of scooping out eyeballs from dead cows?

I wonder who even wonders
about such gross stuff.

Penelope, aka Major Pain in the Butt, today

decided to wear the most fancy and most expensive-looking brand-name knockoff shirt I've ever seen. Not to mention it was so white I had to almost fake pretend to put on sunglasses just to look at her.

She completely and udderly (haha, get it? Sorry, cow) sabotaged me by making me have to be the scalpel person who cuts into the eyeball. What kind of person does that to you? SHE was supposed to cut and I was supposed to squirm and eek and look away from all the grossness.

So I'm mad, and who tries to make a person with a scalpel mad, right? So of course I'm not paying attention and make the incision right in the squishy part of the eyeball, which I'm sure was not one of the instructed parts to cut, and eye juice spurts everywhere!

Okay, not really everywhere, but everywhere that counts. Like right on Penelope's brighter-than-white outfit.

guilty of committing an act of non-cuteness

If anyone knows how to scream like a girl who is getting attacked by zombies in one of those horror movies, it's her. And if anyone knows how to laugh like they're at the funniest stand-up comedy show in the world, it's the class.

She glares at me while her face turns a shade of red that matches my toenail polish. "New York Apple," to be exact.

"Freak," she says as she stomps out of the classroom. Probably to the bathroom to wash up, but I'm hoping she'll just get sucked down the toilet.

MIDDLEBROOKE MIDDLE SCHOOL BLOGGER:

BREAKING NEWS FROM THE

BEST BLOG IN THE WORLD. EVER.

Students in the News: *Is* there anyone who DIDN'T notice an eye juice spatter pattern on P's outfit in the shape of a cow eyeball? Word has it that P has quite a temper, and likes to take it out on poor non-living animals and their organs.

Parents in the News: A.E.'s mom possesses many powers, including psychicness. She can read minds and also figure out what you're going to do before you do it. So don't do it around A.E.! Plus, her mom's ability might be transferable.

Posted by: The Blogtastic Blogger

FRIDAY

19

I'm so grounded! And dead! And . . . and . . . in trouble!

   I have detention and my parents, when they find out, will ground me for life.

If I were a cat, they would ground me
for all nine of my lives.

   And it's not even like it was my fault. Not really. I forgot to put my cell phone in my locker and it rang during class. My phone ring should have been masked by all the laughter that was still going on after Penelope left the room due to the unfortunate eye juice incident. I say should have because TGBE, who sits right next me, yelled out, "Hey, whose phone is ringing?"

I didn't even recognize the number that called me. I should call it back then hang up as soon as the person answers to see if I recognize the voice. There's only one thing stopping me from making that call. And that's my phone. See, there's the slight problem of my phone was taken away by the teacher and I can't get it back until my mom claims it. But then I still won't get it back because I'll be grounded forever with no phone.

And Nona will kick me in my throat if I can't talk to her on the phone anymore because of something stupid I did.

Of course my mom finds out in no time that I have detention. She finds me between classes just to tell me that she knows and we will "talk about it later." That's the worst. It's like parents want you to worry about your punishment for as long as possible before finally telling you what your punishment is.

FRIDAY AFTER SCHOOL... IN DETENTION

I wasn't really sure what to expect in detention, but I definitely didn't expect to hear anything gossipy.

But guess who just happened to get detention on precisely the same day?

Mia.

Coincidence? I think not. And guess what else? Andrew just happens to have detention too. I bet he purposefully got detention so he could tell Mia he likes me. I'm glad I get to witness it.

Mia St. Claire, trying to suddenly act human, leans toward Kylie, the girl sitting right in front of me, and whispers in her ear. And it was one of those loudish whispers that could be heard even if you were more than an ear distance away.

"Isn't he the cutest?" she asks in her most angelic-type loud whisper (gag!).

Apparently I need to send word to Andrew ASAP that Mia St. Claire is not over him like he is of her. I shot a super-quick glance at Andrew, who evidently didn't hear, or isn't paying attention. Or both.

Kylie says, "Oh yeah, Andrew IS cute."

Mia, the rich copycat that she is, shakes her head with a huge smile on her face. "No, not him. HIM."

I follow her very-well-manicured finger beyond Andrew to . . .

Smelly Smelt? I think all her richness and beauty have finally affected her brain.

Kylie skips past Smelly Smelt to the boy behind him. "Mike?"

Mike Sprat. Yep, Nona's biggest crush since forever.

Aha! I knew it. I knew what I heard was very true and correct. It's like Mia St. Claire isn't satisfied by going after MY boyfriend. Now she wants to go after Nona's. She plans to take us all down and form her own little boy army with OUR boyfriends so that she can run the school. I listen carefully.

Kylie: I heard Mike Sprat has a disease.

Mia: What? What disease?

Kylie: Spititus.

Mia: Spit what? What's that?

Kylie: Every time he likes a girl and talks to her, he spits all over her. It's like his spitness is one with his words. There's no controlling it. And sadly, no cure.

Mia: Well, I don't care if he has Spititus. He's still cute. And really nice. I talked to him yesterday but he didn't spit on me, so I guess he doesn't like me.

Nona drowning in a spit sea of love.
What girl wouldn't be jealous?

And at that same exact moment, I swear I heard her say under her breath, "yet." Which really, it shouldn't much surprise me in the least because that's a very Mia St. Claire thing to say.

OTHER GOSSIPY THINGS I HEARD IN DETENTION

1. Nona is mad at me for blogging about her and Mike.

2. Penelope is WAY down on the popularity scale according to Mia St. Claire, who happened to tell this to Math Cheater Megan. I guess Mia thinks Penelope ratted her out about Mike. Which leads to gossip item number 3 . . .

3. Penelope is THE Blogtastic Blogger. I know, I can hardly

grasp this myself. I mean, who would've thought Penelope would turn out to be the anonymous voice behind the ever so almost-popular blog? Wink, wink.

So Sunturday turned out to be a bust. It was so non-fun, especially being Nona-free all weekend. I've tried calling her to apologize, but I think she's screening my calls.

This is Nona's voice mail. I am not screening my calls, but if you're Sofia don't leave a message.

And the worst part of Sunturday? Penelope came over to help write our dead science report on cow eyeballs. I had been kind of avoiding her since the eye juice spatter incident but she's been kind of not avoiding me and not even being her usual mean self. It was her suggestion to come over. Then I figured out why: I did all the writing while she filed her already manicured nails.

I was actually angry enough to have the nerve to ask her why she even bothered coming over in the first place. And you know what she said? She said, "If I didn't, then you would say I didn't participate."

But doesn't participate mean actually doing some participating? There's no way I'm going to do all the work and let her get the grade for it. I'll ask Mr. Q on Monday if I can switch partners.

I don't think Penelope likes drama that she doesn't create, because when I told her I would do this, she said, "You can't threaten me, freak."

And instead of storming out of my house and making a huge grand exit, she went into the bathroom first.

The only good thing that even came out of this Sunturday is that my parents actually showed me a reasonable side of them that was totally wonderful. They said they weren't happy about my detention, but they know I'm "a good kid and won't let it happen again." They gave me my phone back but took away texting privileges for a week. Which in all reality isn't that bad because Nona doesn't have a phone to text with and I really don't text my other friends that much.

Oh yeah, and the number that called me that got me sent to detention in the first place? I pulled my cell out of my pocket and pressed CALL BACK. A minute later Penelope comes out holding her phone. "Why are you calling me? You're so weird."

"You called me that day in class?" I ask her.

"Yeah, you really shouldn't leave your phone in your backpack for everyone to see."

"I can't believe you made me get detention."

"I can't believe you're such a geek."

And with that, she storms out of my house.

It was the kind of storm like in those movies that wipe out half the world.

MONDAY

22

Good news: Mr. Q allowed me to end my partnership with Penelope when I told him I did all the work and she refused to help. We each have to do the project separately, though, which sucks for her because I'm keeping the full report I already wrote and she's forced to do actual work.

Is it so wrong that this made me bust out with a happy dance?

As soon as I see Nona, I dash over to her locker. She's been avoiding me for way too long.

Me: You can't avoid me forever.

Nona: I can try.

Me: But you don't want to. We're BFFs.

Nona: BFFs aren't mean and don't do behind-the-back blogging.

Me: I know I shouldn't have done that. I wasn't thinking. And I'm sorry.

Nona: How sorry are you?

Me: I promise never to blog about you again. And I'll give you my dessert at lunch.

Nona: Forgiven.

Our fights are never usually that bad, but this was the longest we've ever gone without speaking. It was horrible being Nona-less. Now that we're friends again, Nona excitedly tells me her wonderful super-exciting news. She got a part in the school play! But it's only a small part. And a non-speaking role. She says everyone has to start somewhere. I tell her I'll be in the front row clapping the loudest after she finishes non-speaking.

Yay, Nona!
Encore!

Then I tell Nona my superific news: So far, absolutely nobody knows it was my blog. Or notebook. Or anything!

My Pre-Blogging Notebook, although stepped on, has gone unread! I tell Nona we should celebrate, but Nona tells me why I shouldn't.

Astonishing horrible news:

Penelope didn't bump off the popularity meter, she gained overnight mass popularity points that gives her an almost lead over Mia St. Claire. And the reason? HER BLOG. Meaning, MY blog. She is way popular because of MY blog. Everyone thinks she's all gutsy and super-übercool now (except for some of the kids that "she" blogged about who are still holding grudges against her). And it almost seems like kids are trying to get on her good side so that she won't blog about THEM. It might still be a fake type of popularity, but . . .

It's. My. Blog.

Maybe I can spread gossip around school that it's not her blog. Or blog that it's not her blog. Or something. Because really, her mass popularity is only temporary and Mia St. Claire won't read the Best Blog in the World if she thinks that backstabber Penelope is THE blogger. Which means everyone else will stop reading it. Which means . . . my plan of ultimate popularity will fail.

And now Penelope thinks she's all way "super-popular" instead of "just popular" and is going head to head with Mia St. Claire (quite literally) by increasing her bow size. However, it's become apparent that Mia St. Claire is aware of this challenge and refuses to let Penelope take over her place on the popularity scale.

Clearly, Mia St. Claire won't go without a fight.

MIDDLEBROOKE MIDDLE SCHOOL BLOGGER:

BREAKING NEWS FROM THE

BEST BLOG IN THE WORLD. EVER.

Students in the News: All bows aside, Penelope is not THE blogger of THIS blog. And no, this is not Penelope pretending not to be Penelope. So Penelope, if you're reading this, stop trying to claim credit for this blog.

   On a side note, the exact identity of the student whose mom is pregnant hasn't been determined yet, though there is some speculation. It's really only a short matter of time before we find out who it is.

              Posted by: The Blogtastic Blogger

TUESDAY 23

Putting my new plan into action, I pull Nona into the girls' room.

Okay, this plan is so totally thought-out and brilliant that it will work. It has to. Nona and I stand by the sink, pretending to be germaphobes, and wash our already clean hands as we have the following conversation.

Me (in loud voice): So, Nona, did you hear about Penelope?

Nona: (nods)

Me (whispering through clenched teeth): You need to say yes!

Nona: Um, yeah.

Me: And isn't that totally untrue?

Nona: (silence. Eyes roll back in her

head. This is her thinking face.
She forgot her line . . . again!)

Me (improvising): Well, just as you

agreed, it is so totally untrue.

(me elbowing Nona in her side)

Nona: Oomph! (She's in pain.)

Me: Yeah, I know who the real

blogger is and it's definitely not

Penelope. Definitely not.

Nona: (shrugs)

At that precise moment, the girls' room door is
thrown open and like a hundred people walk in
(okay, five). I watch in pure astonishment as they
each go into a stall and this brings me to the most

surprising and horrible realization. All the stalls were completely empty.

Nobody. Heard. Us.

Maybe I wouldn't have failed at this realization if I had paid more attention. And if we'd done a shoe check.

ALWAYS perform the shoe check. And ALWAYS look especially for the really expensive although not-so-cute kind.

I grab Nona's arm and pull her out of the girls' room. And guess who's there?

A) Loud Mom   B) Embarrassing Mom

C) Teacher Mom   D) All of the above

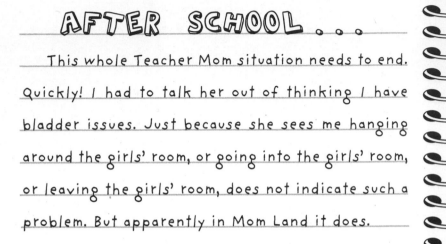

AFTER SCHOOL . . .

This whole Teacher Mom situation needs to end. Quickly! I had to talk her out of thinking I have bladder issues. Just because she sees me hanging around the girls' room, or going into the girls' room, or leaving the girls' room, does not indicate such a problem. But apparently in Mom Land it does.

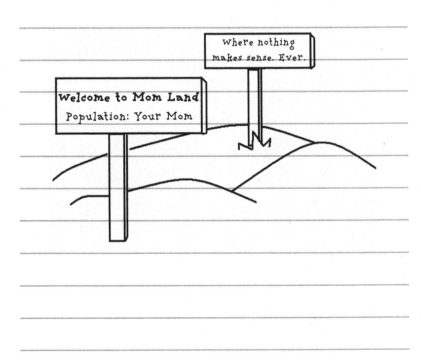

Welcome to Mom Land
Population: Your Mom

Where nothing makes sense. Ever.

LATER AFTER SCHOOL . . .

I still felt bad for blogging about Nona behind her back. I offered her unlimited usage of my cell phone as a way to say I was sorry. But she declined. And she also claims to not be jealous of my phone. She said she has cellphoneaphobia, because one time she talked on her mom's cell for almost two hours and her ear turned bright red and felt like it would burn right off her head. I told her the same thing happens when she eats ketchup, so it's probably more of an allergy and less of a phobia.

OTHER PHOBIAS THAT DON'T MAKE SENSE

Stasibasiphobia:

Fear of walking

Infants have this fear.

Thaasophobia:

Fear of sitting

Now, if you have have this AND stasibasiphobia, you're in real trouble.

Ablutophobia:

Fear of bathing

I know people like this.

Bromidrophobia:

Fear of body smells

These people don't get along with the ablutophobics.

So I guess everyone is convinced now that Penelope is not THE Blogtastic Blogger. Hmmm, I wonder if my blog had any part in that. Everyone is convinced the blogger is a girl. But the blogger could just as easily be a boy.

A boy could very easily eavesdrop in the girls' room by discreetly holding a cup up to the door and listening.

As the blog clearly indicates, the blogger has a strong dislike for Mia St. Claire, and any boy could very easily dislike her. Right? RIGHT?

Boys are very easily as gossipy as girls.

Nona and I post the most creative blog post yet. And it wasn't even that hard to write.

MIDDLEBROOKE MIDDLE SCHOOL BLOGGER:

BREAKING NEWS FROM THE

BEST BLOG IN THE WORLD. EVER.

I don't know about you guys, but today after I ate my lunch, I burped a whole lot.

Then I wore my stinky socks for the third time this week and trampled in mud. I got very dirty and burped some more and refused to take a shower. I even saw M.St.C. and almost barfed because she is so not cute. But even if I did barf, it would be cool because you know how us guys like puking and gross stuff.

Posted by: The Blogtastic Boy Blogger

Blog Comment by Anon Student 1: Why would you want to get dirty?

Blog Comment by Advisor Mr. A: Be careful when blogging about other students and saying mean things that can't be taken back. This is a warning.

Blog Comment by Anon Student 2: LOL guys are gross!

WEDNESDAY

24

As I was coming out of the girls' room, Penelope pounces and points a finger at me all accusingly and in an even more accusingly tone says, "It was you!"

I just look back at her all dumb-like because that's how she's acting. Not to mention she's making my head confused since I haven't the slightest idea what she is accusing me of.

I guess she takes my silence as admittance because she then nods all crazy like one of those bobbleheads stuck to a car dashboard. "You're THE blogger."

If she had been one of those bobbleheads stuck to the dash, I would've slammed on the brakes and knocked her on the floor.

Or I could build a springy-neck
Penelope doll and just pretend.

"Am not," I tell her so matter-of-factly that I
nearly convince myself.

"I know you are, Barfia."

Hey, she SO can't use that name! That's
Andrew's love name for me. That's like plagiarism!

"Am not," I repeat.

She keeps talking like I care.

"Really? Then why didn't I see you in the girls'
room that day I was talking to Mia? You know,
when you had toilet paper stuck to your shoe. And

I know no one else knew about Mia's secret crush."

"Oh please, everyone knew." I try to sound very confident, which I am the total opposite of right now because I've been totally found out and I can't let that happen!

Penelope waves her finger at me. "Then why aren't you blogged about much?"

I shrug. "Guess I'm not very newsworthy."

"And is it just a coincidence that Mia St. Claire, the one person you don't like, is mentioned all the time?"

"What?" I try to say without gagging.

The scowl on Penelope's face shows proof of disbelief. Is my dislike really that obvious?

"Whatever! I'll find a way to prove it." And with that, Penelope leaves me stunned, in the hallway. What do I do now?

AFTER SCHOOL . . .

Even after almost fully recovering from the Penelope incident earlier, my brain went all stupid on me again. One minute I had my notebook, the next minute . . . POOF! It was gone. Just like that.

I told Nona it must have been Andrew or Mia or Penelope who sneakily took it out of my backpack when I wasn't paying attention (which is practically never). Nona pointed out that they don't know I have the notebook so why would they look for it in my backpack? Except Penelope might have realized I was going through her backpack that one day in dead science class and did the same snooping thing to me.

So with my mind already confused and now even more jumbled and horribly terribly upset, I set off a series of chain reactions. It went something like this:

After school I forget (so unlike me!) my geography book in my locker. After I grab it, I head to the girls' room (totally non-gossip related) to wash my face since it's all red and blotchy from me being all worried and stressed and paranoid.

And that's when it happened.

A boy in the girls' room!

Okay, not really a boy, but a man. Okay, not just a man, but one of the after-school janitors. I think. He's dressed very casually (jeans and a T-shirt) like some of the janitors I've seen around after school. Plus, there's a WET FLOOR sign on the ground, which would clearly indicate he probably just mopped.

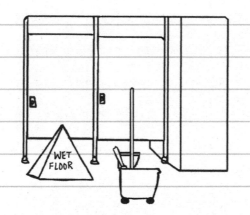

See? If that doesn't say guilty of mopping,
I don't know what does.

And then I see it. In his hand. MY notebook!

Mr. Old Janitor Man (OJM) stole my notebook! Before I can say anything, he says something that totally catches me by surprise:

OJM (holding my notebook): I'll get out of your way. Second time I've found this notebook here.

Me: Um, yeah? Really? (What I'm actually thinking is WHAT? This is the second time you stole my notebook?)

OJM: You would think someone who writes things about other people would be more careful.

Me: Uh, yes. Of course. People can be so careless. (WHAT? HE read MY notebook? I could so die!)

OJM: Yeah, whoever Sofia Becker is sure likes to blog.

Me: Oh, well, I think I know who she is, so I can give the notebook back to her.

OJM: Yeah, Sofia Becker sure doesn't seem to like my daughter much.

And with that, OJM leaves the girls' room, just as my jaw hits the floor.

clink!!

THURSDAY

25

gossip from the girls' Room

Tomorrow is Mia St. Claire's birthday. I'm really surprised she can sound so happy considering she's so poor. Maybe she has a better attitude than I thought.

MAJOR DILEMMA

I've never felt so wonderful/terrible in my life.

Wonderfulness: I could totally take down Mia St. Claire and wipe her right off the popularity meter altogether. Her dad is the janitor! No wonder she never talks about her parents. Actually, I only assume this because she never really talks to me, period. All it would take is one simple blog and that would be it. Almost in fact too easy.

Terribleness: Her dad probably told her I am THE blogger. And she is debating with herself when to bring me further down. I'll be so off the popular meter, I'll have no chance of EVER regaining popularity points. Not even in eighth grade. But she must know that I know who her dad is, which is why she probably hasn't said anything yet. So what if I out her on my blog and then she decides to out me? It would be social suicide. I can't do that. But I can't not do that either.

I have no choice. I call up my anger ball of a best friend for some friendly angry advice. Which, by the way, is way more safe than talking to her in person with all the noticeably crabby days she's been having lately.

THE EVOLVING CRABBINESS OF NONA BOWS

Little Crabby — like a "failed a math test but will study extra hard for the next one" bad day.

Pretty Crabby — complete with eye twitch and look of total confusion. Comes with caution warning: "Don't even sneeze in my direction!"

Full-Blown Crabby — could it get any worse? Wear protective suit and plastic goggles. May unexpectedly strike at any given moment without warning!

Nona tried to solve my dilemma in one word. Actually three words. And they were spoken as very angry words:

Take. Mia. Down.

I think Nona is still very upset over Mia trying to steal Mike Sprat from her. Although I must admit Mia is now ignoring Andrew, which makes me feel all warm and happy inside. But nobody needs to know that.

My usual happy, flowery friend Nona has gone from angry to way angry to totally angry in such a short time. And to think this is all because of a boy! I hope Mia isn't over Mike too, because then she'll go running back to Andrew, who, by the way, hasn't been talking to her much at all.

Notice the presence of the skull flower?
Only angry people wear skulls.

So really, I find myself questioning whether I should really take Mia St. Claire down. Crazy, right? I guess I really am capable of being a caring and nice person to someone as horrible as Mia. And it might not even have to do with Mia being unfortunately so poor and non-rich. Which is the total opposite of what I originally thought.

And for the moment, I should probably temporarily forget all the stuff she's done to me. After all, poor Mia probably gets all her clothes and jewelry and richy-looking bows from a second-hand store for wannabe rich girls.

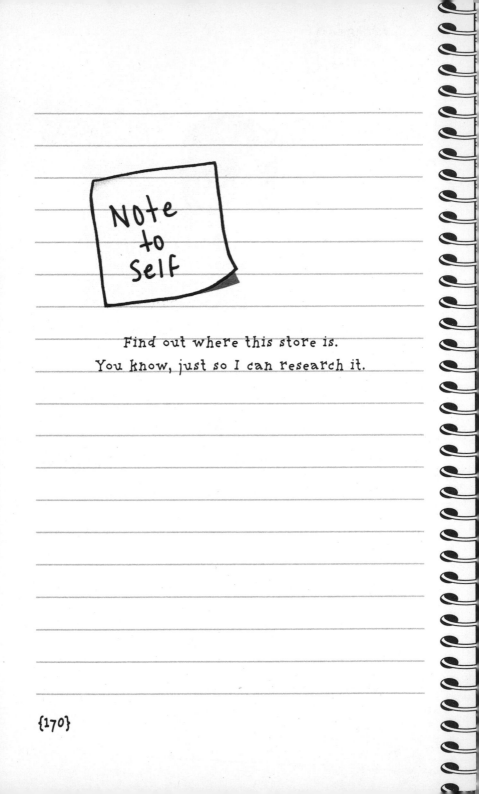

Note
to
Self

Find out where this store is.
You know, just so I can research it.

MIDDLEBROOKE MIDDLE SCHOOL BLOGGER:

BREAKING NEWS FROM THE

BEST BLOG IN THE WORLD. EVER.

Students in the News: M.St.C. wore the absolute cutest most expensive-looking bow ever today. Also C.J. broke out in hives while giving a book presentation in class. Who says classwork isn't stressful?

Posted by: The Blogtastic Blogger

FRIDAY

26

Today is Mia's birthday. I bet poor unfortunate Mia can't afford a party. Or cake and ice cream. Which makes me think of my next totally nice and caring action.

And it wasn't even a box of worms or anything smelly gross like one might expect or suggest (not saying names, but Nona did), which is probably why Mia St. Claire made the face that she did when she opened the box.

{172}

Mia whispered a quiet little "thank you" like she could hardly believe it (the beautifulness probably took her breath away), then the stink face disappeared and she flashed me the biggest smile ever. You know, that one reserved for special occasions.

Her smile really is magical and made me
feel all warm and fuzzy inside.

I knew she'd love it! I told her I made the bow for her myself. Now she can look even more rich, thanks to me and my selfless caring self. I can't wait to see her wear it!

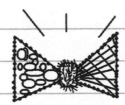

retro plaid. bead trim made with the awesomeness of a bedazzler. chic fur trim. super-cute polka dots.

SUNTUPDAY

27 & 28

Mom and Dad announce another sit-down talk. My brain rattles through all the horrible things this talk could possibly lead to, then I come to the most horrible conclusion: Mom is becoming a permanent teacher at my school.

Dad must've thought I was having a seizure because when my eyes rolled back in my head and I saw "the light" he grabbed my shoulder and asked if I was okay.

even though the light was only from the very high voltage of our tacky table lamp

For some reason my dad—who is usually always so very understanding of my feelings—has a huge smile on his face. So does my mom. Maybe it's not bad news after all.

Mom is the one who decidedly, and very loudly, breaks the news to me.

I'M HAVING A BABY!

All the brain numbness has finally caught up to me and affected my hearing. I swore my mom just said "I'm having a baby."

Then Mom rubs her flat stomach. Like there's actually a baby in there or something. Which can't be true because her stomach is too flat to have anything but lunch fit in there. Dad tells me she's four months along. And they want to be surprised so they aren't finding out the baby's sex.

I just stare in total disbelief, not sure what to say. Especially since I'M the girl that everyone has been talking about. I'm the one whose life is going to be ruined. And who's going to be unspoiled. And forgotten about.

So when I ask her why she told everyone at school before me, she acts all surprised like she didn't know. She blames it on Macy's mom, who saw her at the doctor's office and must've told Macy, who told one person, who told another person, until it was overheard. By me.

I've totally ruined myself with all my baby blogs! Except, I can still be saved. I mean, nobody has to ever know. I just won't mention it. Unless Macy tells everyone it's MY mom. Plus my mom won't be teaching at my school much longer so really, maybe it will all just go away.

But for me it will never go away. I'm going to be a big sister. I hate the thought of another person coming into our family. I mean, it's always just been me and Mom and Dad. But also, I'm getting older, practically a teen. So maybe Mom and Dad need someone else to focus on since I'm not a baby anymore. And maybe they'll finally stop treating me like a baby too.

For now, I just won't think about it and I'll just focus on my super-successful blog and find something to steer everyone far, far away from baby blankets and (ugh!) diapers.

MIDDLEBROOKE MIDDLE SCHOOL BLOGGER:

BREAKING NEWS FROM THE

BEST BLOG IN THE WORLD. EVER.

Students in the News: As it turns out, there is no student with a pregnant mother. It must've all been a rumor.

On a side note, M.St.C. received a lavishly styled bow as a birthday gift.

Teachers in the News: Mr. J went home with food poisoning. Did he eat the cafeteria food?

Posted by: The Blogtastic Blogger

MONDAY 29

Nona has given me the silent anger treatment ever since Mia and I bonded over the bow, which, BTW, I gained like a ton of popularity points for too! Nona's really just jealous. But I told her I wouldn't forget her when I become popular. In fact, I would help her become popular too! Isn't that what a BFF is for?

OTHER THINGS BEST FRIENDS ARE FOR...

What do you call a snail on a ship?

What?

A SNAILOR !!

Ah ha haha !

laughing at jokes that might be completely stupid

showing appreciation with matching name tags
(you know, since friendship bracelets
are so overrated)

trusting each other

I finally need to vent about my mom's latest news, so I pull Nona over to a quiet spot to talk to her, which just happens to be by the lost and found box.

It's really amazing how many things are lost and never claimed. Even by unoriginal owners of the stuff. Like, say you're missing a sock. What are you going to do? Go to the Lost and Found! Problem solved. Or, you're in a bind and need . . . a hat? One earring? You'll find it here.

But what's also amazing is how some of this stuff was ever lost in the first place. I mean, who "loses" their T-shirt? Oops, my tee flew off my body and landed somewhere unknown.

OTHER THINGS THAT WERE PROBABLY "LOST" ON PURPOSE

- Elmo lunch bag (Why is it always Elmo? What about Cookie Monster?)
- Sunglasses with one lens (great for a pirate in summertime. Arrr!)
- Retainer (eww!)
- Dora underwear (um, seriously?)

Nona acts like the news isn't horrible. In fact, she was totally excited. She said she's always wanted a little brother or sister. She even pointed out all the pros and cons of having a baby brother/sister and it turns out the pros weigh more.

Pros:

- Babies are cute and adorable and make little gurgly noises.
- Big-sis advantages, such as helping with the baby, using babysitting as an excuse when I need one, and protecting him or her.
- I'll never be lonely. It's like having a pet, but better. Sorry, Sam Sam!
- I won't be an only child anymore—which means Mom

and Dad probably w.

strict with me anymore.

- I get to be bossy.
- I can probably help name the baby. At the very least, stop my mom from naming the baby after furniture.

Cons:

- Smelly diapers and crying at night (solution—nose plug and earplugs!)
- Parents won't make same mistakes with baby. As the firstborn, I'm kind of like a guinea pig.
- Parents will probably give most of their attention to the baby at first.

IN THE
GIRLS' ROOM...

It shouldn't have come as a surprise when Mia decided to talk to me in the girls' room today. Us almost-popular people like to schmooze in the girls' room, you know. However, quite sadly, no one else was in there so I only gained like one popularity point instead of eight. But still, one is better than minus one!

Mia: Thanks again for the bow. (Even though she is regretfully not wearing it.) I wore it at my party last night. Everyone talked about it (because it was so wonderful).

Me: Oh, you had a party? (She says "party" but probably means a get-together for poor kids.)

Mia: Yeah. Sorry I couldn't invite you, but all the seats in the limo were already filled. (She says "limo" but probably really means used minivan.)

Me: That's okay. I totally get it!

Mia: By the way, your mom is super-great!

Me: Um, my mom? (If I were sipping soda, it would've spit through my nose at this point.)

Mia: I had no idea she backpacked through Spain. And she makes class so interesting.

Me: Oh, well . . .

She must be talking about someone else's Teacher Mom.

Mia: And don't worry, I get the whole parent-working-at-school thing. It can be so embarrassing, right?

Me: Totally!

Mia: Yeah, like last week my dad had to work here at school. But luckily, it was after school so NOBODY saw him.

Me: Oh really? (I fake astonishment. Have we bonded so much that she is now currently telling me all her deepest darkest secrets that she dares not even tell her best friends? And yay, it appears her dad didn't mention the fact that he found my notebook.)

Mia: Yeah, he had to inspect the school. Some kind of issue, I guess. No biggie, though.

Me: Oh, your dad is the janitor? (Acting dumb will only encourage her to tell me more. Especially since I mentioned janitor.)

Mia: Janitor? (She laughs. Hard. Must be nervous laughter.) Oh, no. My dad owns this huge chain of successful inspection companies, Claire Industries. Middlebrooke uses my dad's company all the time. Anyway, that's the bell. Talk to you later!

And just like that, Mia St. Claire saunters out of the girls' room and leaves me, much in the same way her dad the non-janitor old man left me the other day—with my jaw on the floor.

It was after school and NOBODY saw him.

TUESDAY 30

It has been THE longest month of my life. Ever. I wish I could retire from school.

Mia is rich again. Boo.

And what would make the longest month ever seem even longer?

More bad news!

Mom (who apparently kept her Spanish skills secret"o") is not a substitute teacher anymore. No longer a part-time embarrassment. Get this—she was offered a full-time teaching position! At my school! I know, I'm completely out of reactions with which to express this.

Mom also keeps bugging me about taking Spanish because it will help me and French isn't as commonly used, and blah blah blah. I told her "je ne parle anglais."

Besides, I need to concentrate on gathering courage to talk to Andrew. You know what he did today? He walked right past me in the hallway. And he talked to me! (Swoon!)

Hey, Barfia!

Nona was serious when she said Mike was yesterday's news. Now she is crushing on Jonathan, a transfer student, who is in drama with her.

Nona excitedly met me by my locker to tell me about this idea she had. She said my mom being pregnant was a great way to stay anonymous. She said if I out myself on my blog about this, then nobody will think that I'm THE blogger, because really, who would out themselves on their very own blog? Nona, in all her smartness, also pointed out that eventually everyone will know about my mom since she'll be a full-time teacher now. If I just blog it now, by next week it should become old news. Plus, she said it would make my blog even more super-popular.

This is a great idea, especially since everyone still thinks the blogger is female, even after my "boy" blog. Although Nona and I are in synchronized agreement that my boy-blogged entry was totally believable.

MIDDLEBROOKE MIDDLE SCHOOL BLOGGER:

BREAKING NEWS FROM THE

BEST BLOG IN THE WORLD. EVER.

HUGE MISTAKE ALERT!! There is in fact a classmate with a pregnant mom. It's sixth grader S. This is a total fact and not just a gossipy rumor. Even though some people think it's hugely embarrassing and her life will be totally ruined now, it appears that S. might actually be excited about the news. Maybe she's just weird. BTW, S.'s mom is now also the permanent Spanish teacher. Rumor has it that the old Spanish teacher went on vacation to Madrid and liked it there so much, he never wanted to come back.

Posted by: The Blogtastic Blogger

WEDNESDAY

31

I think I'm through blogging mean things about Mia. Not that we're friends or ever will be, but it really sucks having people talk about you, even if you don't know it's you at the time.

and even if you find the wonderful bow
that you gave someone in the lost and found,
totally unappreciated

her loss, my cuteness gain

Another confession: I'm totally dreading Monday.
By then everyone will have found out that my mom
is pregnant.

Maybe I'll have to hide out in the girls' room.
Not stake out, but actually hide. I'll even wear
earplugs if I need to so that my precious ears won't
accidentally overhear anything.

Even though I am an excellent lip-reader.

It will probably take about a thousand and one
times longer to get popular than I originally
thought. But I guess I can blog about things that
aren't so gossipy. I mean, I'm sure I could still find

interesting things to keep kids totally wanting to read.

Like for instance, it's been said (not gossip, Mr. Allen told us) that we might be getting a foreign exchange student. That would be super-cool. Especially if it was a boy. And if he comes from some really awesome country like Egypt or France. Or Iceland.

Oh, and it would be way cool if I became friends with him, and he became friends with Andrew, and then I could ask him if Andrew ever talks about me. Unless the foreign exchange boy doesn't speak English.

I wonder if Andrew ever really <u>does</u> talk about me to his friends. Or what his friends say about Mia when she isn't around. Or if boys really are as gossipy as girls (which I suspect).

Hmmm, I wonder what goes on in the boys' room. . . .

ABOUT THE AUTHOR

ROSE COOPER is a children's book writer and illustrator and a self-taught artist. Her artwork can be seen in galleries and at art fairs and festivals. Writing for children gives her the perfect excuse to keep in touch with her inner child and never really grow up. She lives in Sacramento, California, with her husband, Carl, and their three boys. You can visit Rose's website at rose-cooper.com.

11.09

DATE DUE			